To Isadora —
A great girl!

Amy Krahow

For my own siblings
Jaime & Betsy

Copyright 2005 Amy Krakow
ISBN-0-9715224-2-1
Illustration Copyright by Steve Williams
graphictraffic@yahoo.com
Illustrations were done in watercolor, pen and ink and colored pencil.
Cover design and layout by James Kosmicki
jkoz@sopris.net
Font is Garamond
Printed in the United States of America by
Walsworth Publishing Company

Wagging Tales Publishing
Box 691
Carbondale, Colorado 81623
amykrakow@hotmail.com

THE Mutt AND THE Monster GO SKIING & SNOWBOARDING

Written by Amy Krakow
Illustrations by Steve Williams

Winter is my favorite time of year. Lucy puts a little oil on my food, I grow a new coat and I get to snowboard every Saturday at Buttermilk Mountain. The only problem is the Mutt gets to come too.

When we go through Crazy T'rain Terrain Park, Lucy always makes me go first and then I have to wait for the Mutt and she takes forever. She always does a face plant off the rails and then she complains that the jumps have scary, giant snow snakes hidden inside of them.

When we go through Devil's Gut tree trail, Lucy always lets the Mutt go first and makes me help her when she wipes out but I always crash into the Mutt because she's so slow. She's afraid monkeys are hanging out in the trees and they'll grab her tail and take her prisoner.

When we go down Lover's Lane, also known as the Toilet Bowl the Mutt always gets flushed down because she forgets to put her goggles on and then she drops a pole and crashes big time and her skis come off. Lucy gets really mad at me because I won't help the Mutt pick everything up.

When we go to Aspen Highlands, Lucy always makes me carry the Mutt's skis all the way up to the top of the Highland Bowl while the Mutt gets to play frisbee with the rescue dogs.

On powder days Lucy takes us to Snowmass and I ride the Big Burn. Sometimes the powder is so deep I can't see a thing. One time I hit this gigantic mogul and flew one hundred feet into the air. I totally rocked until Lucy yelled at me. I didn't know that big mogul was really the Mutt buried under the snow.

When it's time for lunch the Mutt gets a humongous grilled sneeze sandwich and Lucy lets her put fifty marshmallows in her hot chocolate while I have to eat a crummy cold sandwich from home.

When Lucy takes us to Aspen Mountain she always lets the Mutt sit next to her on the gondola while I have to sit on the other side next to complete strangers.

One of my favorite runs on Aspen Mountain is Corkscrew Gulley. It feels like I'm on a mini half pipe and I pretend I'm in the Olympics and I win the gold medal but Lucy hardly ever lets me ride it because it makes the Mutt dizzy.

At the end of the day Lucy always lets the Mutt pick her favorite run and makes me follow her. The Mutt always goes down really boring trails with no trees, bumps or jumps. It's so embarrassing. I feel like a real wimp!

Sometimes it feels like Lucy loves the Mutt more than me. Even in winter.

Yeah…. yeah…. yeah. That's what the Monster says but here's the "real" story.
Winter is my favorite season! Lucy lets me sleep on a goose down quilt, she buys me pretty ski suits imported from Sweden and I get to ski every Saturday at Buttermilk Mountain. The only problem is the Monster gets to come too.

When we go through the terrain park the Monster always shows off. She likes to ride the rails and do 360's over double black diamond jumps. When I try to ride the rails I always land on my butt and the Monster laughs at me and Lucy never ever hears her.

When we go through Toad's Road tree trail the Monster cuts right in front of me and makes me fall down. One time I even kissed a tree!

When I ski down the Toilet Bowl the Monster rides her board so fast that she kicks up a ton of snow and it makes me wipe out big time.

When we go to Aspen Highlands I have to wait forever for the Monster to get to the top of the Bowl. She really needs to work out.

One time I let Chase, the rescue dog, bury me under a foot of snow but when she tried to dig me out she couldn't find her shovel. The Monster had stolen it.

On powder days Lucy takes us to Snowmass and I ski the Big Burn. Sometimes the powder is so deep I have to wear my snorkel just to breathe. One time a snow snake grabbed my ski boot and I did a face plant and the Monster snowboarded right over me.

When it's time for lunch Lucy gives the Monster a gourmet sandwich she packed especially for her while I have to wait in line forever to buy my lunch and then I always burn my tongue on my hot chocolate.

When Lucy takes us to Aspen Mountain she makes me sit next to her on the gondola because she thinks I might get car sick. The Monster gets to ride on the other side where she gets to sit next to famous movie stars.

One of my favorite runs on Aspen Mountain is Dipsy Doodle. It's great for cruising but Lucy hardly ever lets me ski it because the Monster is too much of a "dude" to cruise.

At the end of the day Lucy always lets the Monster pick her favorite run and makes me follow her. The Monster always goes down the steepest, bumpiest, hardest trail with a zillion trees and monkeys. I'm really tired and my paws are killing me in these ski boots.

Sometimes it feels like Lucy loves the Monster more than me. Even in winter.

Kids Comment on THE Mutt AND THE Monster

"Your stories are incredible. They make me laugh, smile and much more."

Madison Higgens

"Thank you for coming to our school. I loved your books. I think the Mutt is cuter but the Monster has a better attitude."

Lexi

"I like the part where the Mutt cannot do as hard of runs as the Monster does like my brother and me."

Kaylene Loo

"When the Mutt kissed a tree it was very funny and I think that if a real dog did that it would be pretty funny too."

Riley Perez

"I like your books because they are funny. My favorite part is when the Mutt kissed the tree because I laughed so hard I almost bursted!"

Kelcee Wissel

"I really like your books. They are funny, silly and they make kids laugh. I can't wait until your new book is published. I can't have a dog because a dog ripped up my mother's favorite shirt and because I am beginning to be allergic to dogs. So we just have nine fish and we don't have room for a horse."

Franny DiPaola

My Dogs
Sometimes it makes me sad to think
about the dogs I've had.
Some were big, some were small,
but I loved them one in all.
I wish I could bring them down,
to take away my sometimes frown.
These dogs will always be in my heart,
even though we are apart.

Will Masters

CANINE COMMENTS

"I'm a dude like the Monster. I love to slide and ride and I don't think it's fair that Lucy makes the Mutt come with us. It's so embarrassing!" P.S. Dogs Rule!!!

Sage-Pointer

"Okay. I know I'm just a cat but I really don't get what the big deal about skiing and snowboarding is. I'll play with my pal Smokey in my sandbox any day."

Nemo-Cat Mutt

"If you ask me I think the Mutt is one terrific skier. Okay so she likes to kick back and cruise a little. What's wrong with that? You would too if you kissed a million trees."

Iggy- Standard Poodle

"One time I rode the chairlift with the Mutt and the Monster and the Monster kept trying to push the Mutt off the chair."

Josie-Mutt

"This is an awesome book! My favorite part is when the Mutt gets hot chocolate with marshmallows. I think all dogs should be able to have hot chocolate and tummy rubs by the fire in the lodge. That's the best part of skiing and snowboarding."

Cirrus-Black Lab   R.E.A.D.

"When I went skiing with the Mutt and the Monster the Mutt kept telling me to watch out for snow snakes and monkeys. I didn't know those animals lived in Colorado."

Otis-Black Lab

Mutt (a.k.a. Sparky) • **Monster (a.k.a. Spooner)**

The real Mutt and Monster love to cross country ski and play in the snow. They would love to ski and snowboard everyday but unfortunately they have to work for a living.

Partial proceeds from this book go to Valley Dog Rescue, an organization in the Roaring Fork Valley that shelters and protects unwanted dogs until they can be adopted. Special thanks to those heroes who have worked endlessly to save the lives of so many animals. To visit their web site go to (*http://welcome.to/vdr*). Having a no kill policy and being a non-profit means that some dogs have to wait for a very long time before they can finally "go home."

For donations please send check or money order to:

Dog Rescue Fund
Bank of Colorado
Box 520
Glenwood Springs, CO 81602
Acct.# 5930047589

Other books by the author:

The Mutt And The Monster

The Mutt And The Monster Go To Mexico (A Bi-lingual book)

To order additional books and/or schedule author school visits, please contact the author at:

amykrakow@hotmail.com

Acknowledgments:

I would like to give a special thanks to two fabulous teachers and friends, Allyson Bella-Dodds and Cathie Farrar for all their help and support during the writing process of the Mutt And Monster series.

Spooner

Monster

This book is also dedicated to my two best friends, Spooner and Sparky.
It is also dedicated to the dogs of my childhood and beyond with whom I've shared a very special love...Lucy, Nicki, Ogian, Kelly and Stonewall.

Sparky

Mutt

"Everyone is born so they can learn how to live a good life, like loving everybody and being nice. Well, dogs already know how to do that, so they don't have to stay as long"

Anonymous